FRIENDS FOREVER

PUFFIN

Map of my woods

This is a map of the woods where I live. You can see who else lives here too. It's in my dad's journal, which I always have with me.

ROCKY ISLAND

OLD BROWN'S ISLAND

MR JEREMY FISHER'S POND

SQUIRREL NUTKIN'S WOOD

MRS TIGGY-WINKLE'S LAUNDRY

Tommy Brock is a badger who loves worms, but hates rabbits!

JEMIMA PUDDLE-DUCK'S
HILLTOP FARM

MR MCGREGOR'S
GARDEN

MR TOD & TOMMY
BROCK'S WOOD

MY BURROW

DR & MRS BOBTAIL'S
BURROW (LILY'S HOME)

TUNNEL
NETWORK

MR BOUNCER'S BURROW
(BENJAMIN'S HOME)

RAVINE

DEEP DARK WOODS

DANDELION FIELD

My friend,
Lily Bobtail.
Whatever the
problem, she's
got the answer.

Benjamin Bunny
is my cousin.
Whatever I do,
he's right behind
me – usually
hiding!

One spring evening, Peter, Lily and Benjamin were hopping home with a stash of delicious freshly picked dandelions.

It was getting dark, and Peter kept stopping and scratching his head.

"I'm sure it's this way . . .
Just round this corner . . .
Um . . .

We're lost!"

he blurted out.

But Lily had an idea.
"Just-in-Case Pocket,
just in case!" she said,
whipping out a telescope.
"We can use the stars
to guide us home!"

"WOW, Lily!"
said Benjamin.
"That's
INCREDIBLE!"

"This way,"

said Lily, hopping off with Benjamin behind her.

"I would have remembered the way in
the end," mumbled Peter, following
them home.

The next morning, Benjamin found
Lily examining a leaf.

"Can I see?"

he asked shyly.
"Will you teach me
about stars and leaves
and things?"

"Yes! Let's go on a nature walk," Lily smiled. "You can borrow my magnifying glass."

Benjamin was **SO** happy he couldn't speak.

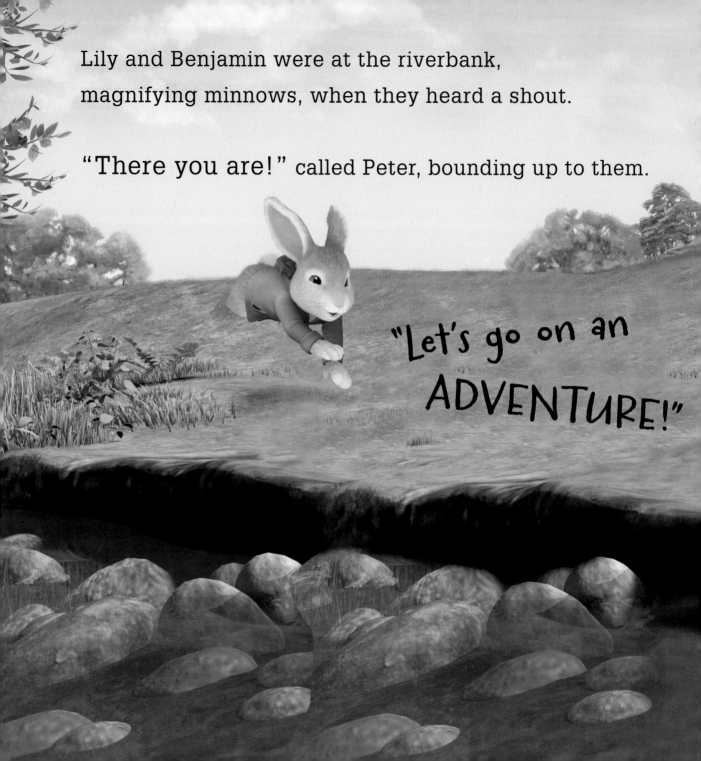

Lily and Benjamin were at the riverbank,
magnifying minnows, when they heard a shout.

"There you are!" called Peter, bounding up to them.

"Let's go on an ADVENTURE!"

"Actually, we're on a nature walk," said Benjamin. "Do you want to come along?"

"All right," said Peter slowly. "Maybe we'll find an adventure on the way . . ."

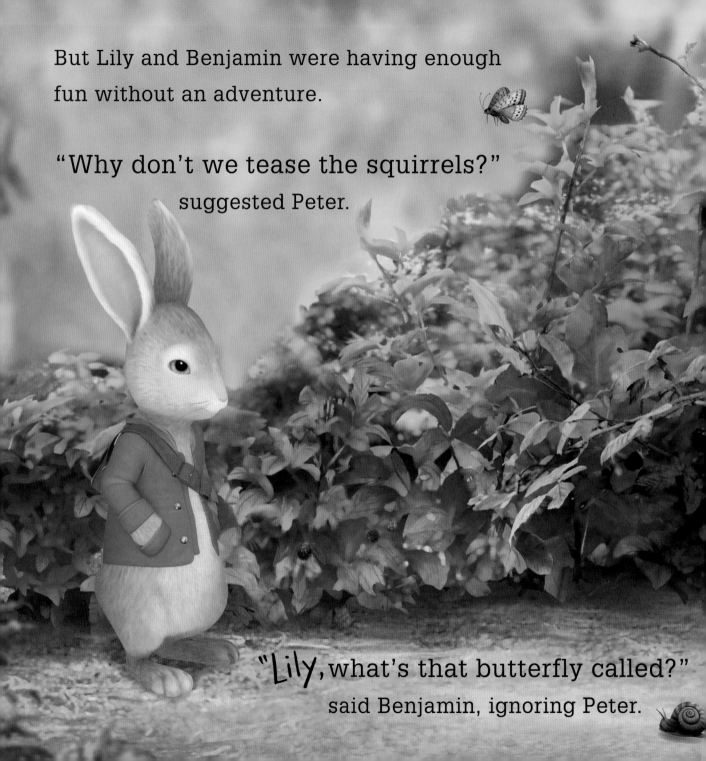

But Lily and Benjamin were having enough fun without an adventure.

"Why don't we tease the squirrels?" suggested Peter.

"Lily, what's that butterfly called?" said Benjamin, ignoring Peter.

"Or we could steal strawberries from Mr Tod?" Peter continued.

"Shhh, Peter, you're scaring the bugs!" hushed Lily.

Peter rolled his eyes. "I just wish this walk was more adventurous!" he muttered.

As they neared Mr McGregor's garden,
Peter started fidgeting, until . . .

"Let's go on a radish raid!" he cried.

"Maybe later?" said Benjamin.
"Peter, come and look at the
leaf Lily has found!"

"I think I'll just go on a radish raid by myself," Peter mumbled sadly.

As he squeezed under the gate into Mr McGregor's garden, Peter forgot all about the nature walk.

He skirted round the edge of the garden and leaped over the cat.

Tugging at some juicy radishes, he heard heavy footsteps running towards him.

"Mr McGregor!"

Peter gasped.

Quick as a flash,
Peter darted through
Mr McGregor's legs
and back through
the gate.

"PHEW!"

Safely out of Mr McGregor's garden, Peter bit into a radish.

"Radishes just don't taste as good without friends to share them with," he sighed, watching Lily and Benjamin chasing a butterfly.

Suddenly, Peter stopped chomping.

"Oh no!"

he gasped.

Lily and Benjamin were running straight towards . . .

. . . Tommy Brock!

"STOP!"

yelled Peter, leaping up . . . just as
Lily and Benjamin crashed straight
into the snoring badger.

"Rabbits!" spat Tommy Brock, shaking his head angrily. "I'll teach you to wake me up!"

"Why don't you pick on someone your own size?" shouted Peter, launching himself between Tommy Brock and his terrified friends.

"Benjamin! Lily! RUN!"

"Grrr! I'll make you ALL into SLIPPERS!" snarled Tommy Brock, swiping at Peter.

The friends raced out of the woods, but
Tommy Brock was very close behind them.

"Catch us if you can!" shouted Peter,
reaching into his satchel.

"Snack time!"

he yelled, throwing the last of Mr McGregor's
radishes into the lumbering badger's path.

"Hey!" grunted Tommy Brock,
as he slipped on the radishes and fell –

CRASH!

The bunnies quickly
scurried away.

"Peter, you saved us!"

said Benjamin, as the bunnies stopped to catch their breath. "But you've lost all your radishes . . ."

"There are plenty more in Mr McGregor's garden," Peter smiled.

"RADISH RAID!"

cheered Lily and Benjamin.

"What about your nature walk?" asked Peter.

"The nature walk was lots of fun," said Lily. "But nothing beats an adventure with all your **BEST FRIENDS.**"

LILY'S JUST-IN-CASE POCKET

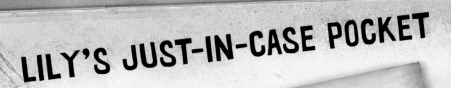

Lily's pocket is full of useful and interesting things. Whenever we're in a tricky situation, Lily's sure to find something in there to get us out of trouble.

Emergency radish supply

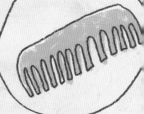

Comb for unpicking tricky knots (and a bunny needs to keep her fur neat!)

Matchbox where Lily keeps her pet ladybird, Florence

Notebook and pencil for lists, plans and sketches

Ball of string

Sock Now THAT shouldn't be in here!

Safety pins

Magnifying glass Lily's most precious possession – for examining nature . . . or finding clues

Elastic bands

That's what **FRIENDS** are for

Though Peter didn't want to join in Lily and Benjamin's game, he proved he was a true friend by helping them when they were in danger.

Can you do something
special for your friends?

YOU COULD:

Pick them a bunch of flowers
or draw them a picture.

Share a favourite toy.

Give them a big hug.

Take them on an adventure!

Then you can be best friends
like Peter, Lily and Benjamin!

CONGRATULATIONS!

FRIENDSHIP SKILLS CERTIFICATE

Awarded to

_____

Age

_____

Lily Bobtail
_____
LILY BOBTAIL
BEST FRIEND EVER

We'll ALWAYS be friends!